Growing Readers

Purchased with Smart Start Funds

To Gloria, Theresa, and Martin.
From my hands to your hands.
—T. R.

Text copyright © 1985 by Bill Martin Jr and John Archambault/Illustrations copyright © 1987 by Ted Rand.
All rights reserved, including the right to reproduce this book or portions thereof in any form.
First published in book form in 1987 by Henry Holt and Company, Inc., 115 West 18th Street, New York, New York 10011.
Published in Canada by Fitzhenry & Whiteside Limited, 195 Allstate Parkway, Markham, Ontario L3R 4T8.

Library of Congress Cataloging-in-Publication Data
Martin Jr, Bill/Here are my hands.
Summary: The owner of a human body celebrates it by pointing out various parts and mentioning their functions,
from "hands for catching and throwing" to "skin that bundles me in."
[1. Body, Human—Fiction.   2. Stories in rhyme]   I. Archambault, John   II. Rand, Ted, ill.   III. Title.
PZ8.3.M418He   1987   [E]   86-25842

ISBN 0-8050-0328-2 (hardcover)                    ISBN 0-8050-1168-4 (paperback)
11   13   15   17   19   20   18   16   14   12   10        13   15   17   19   20   18   16   14

First Owlet paperback edition, 1989                    Printed in the United States of America

# Here Are My Hands

## By Bill Martin Jr and John Archambault
## Illustrated by Ted Rand

Henry Holt and Company
New York

Here are my hands
for catching and throwing.

Here are my feet
for stopping and going.

Here is my head

for thinking and knowing.

Here is my nose
for smelling and blowing.

Here are my eyes

for seeing and crying.

Here are my ears
for washing and drying.

Here are my knees
for falling down.

Here is my neck
for turning around.

Here are my cheeks
for kissing and blushing.

Here are my teeth

for chewing and brushing.

Here is my elbow,
my arm, and my chin.

And here is my skin
that bundles me in.

← BC

GR